TRANSFORMERS
REVENGE OF THE FALLEN

Rise of the Decepticons

JS

First published in the UK by HarperCollins Children's Books in 2009

1 3 5 7 9 10 8 6 4 2

ISBN-13: 978-0-00-731085-2

TRANSFORMERS ©2009 Hasbro. All Rights Reserved. © 2009 DreamWorks, LLC and Paramount Pictures Corporation. All Rights Reserved.

A CIP catalogue record for this title is available from the British Library.

Printed and bound in China

TRANSFORMERS
REVENGE OF THE FALLEN

Rise of the Decepticons

Adapted by Jennifer Frantz
Illustrations by Marcelo Matere
Based on the Screenplay by
Ehren Kruger & Alex Kurtzman & Roberto Orci

HarperCollins *Children's Books*

The evil Megatron lost
his last battle
with Optimus Prime,
the leader of the Autobots.

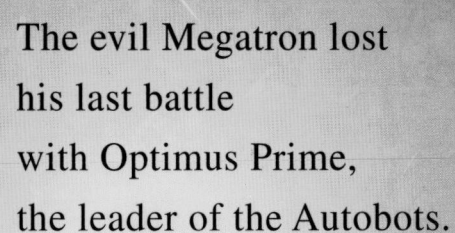

Megatron is the leader of the Decepticons. Decepticons and Autobots are sworn enemies.

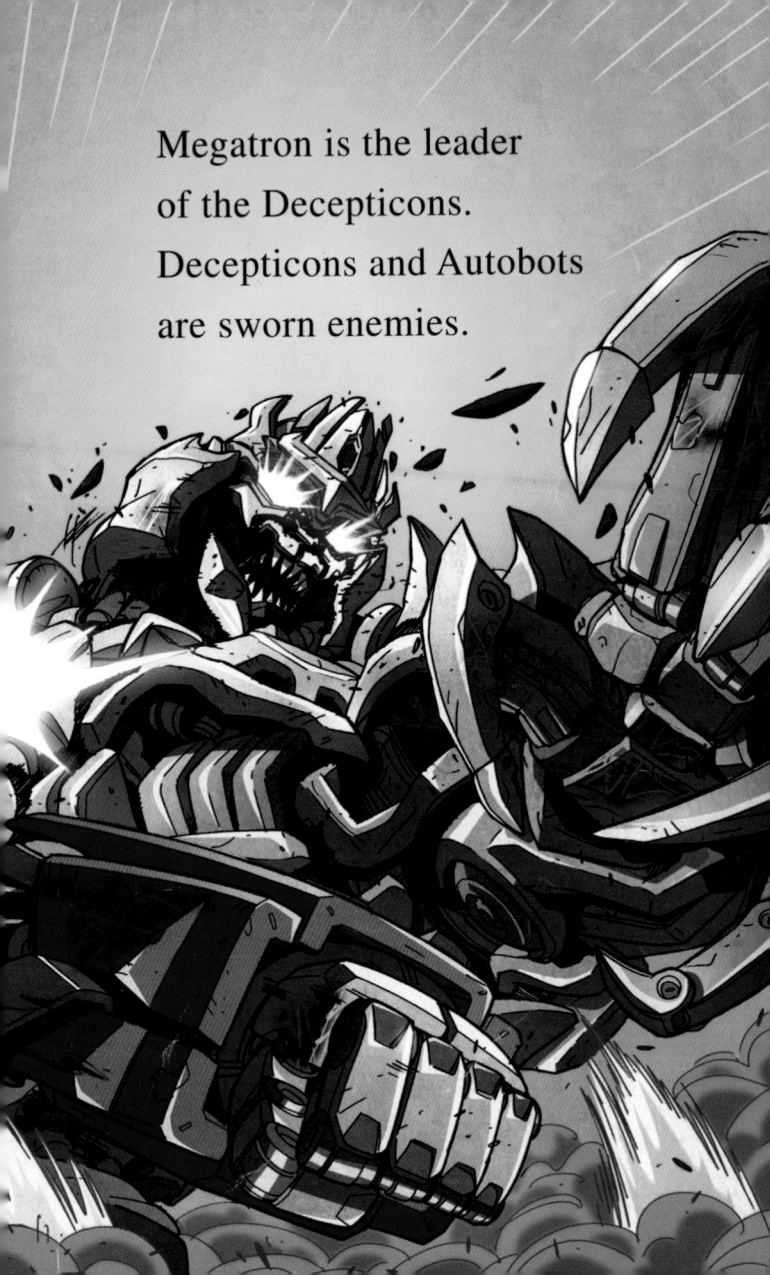

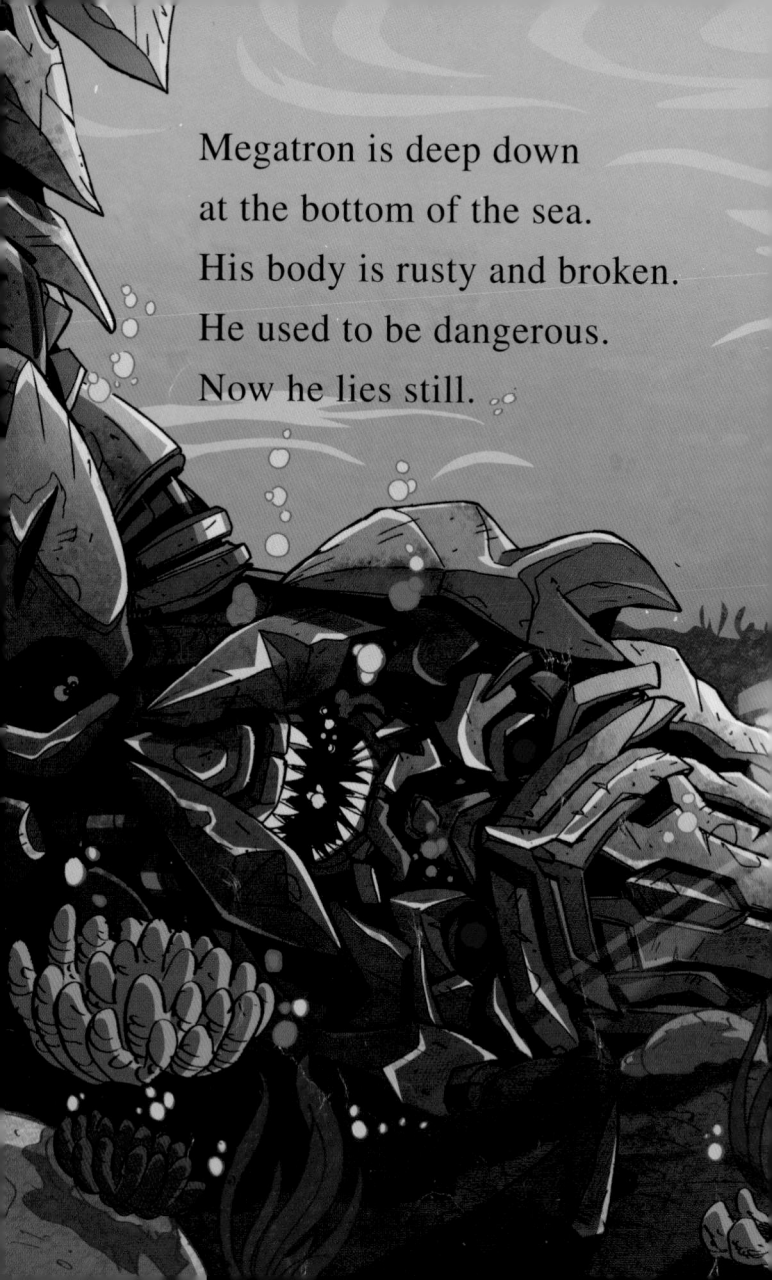

Megatron is deep down
at the bottom of the sea.
His body is rusty and broken.
He used to be dangerous.
Now he lies still.

Humans don't want Megatron
to rise up again.
The Navy watches over him
with submarines.

Megatron's Decepticon forces want to get their leader back. Soundwave hacks into the Navy computers.

Soundwave finds all the top secret
information he needs.
Now the Decepticons can make a plan.

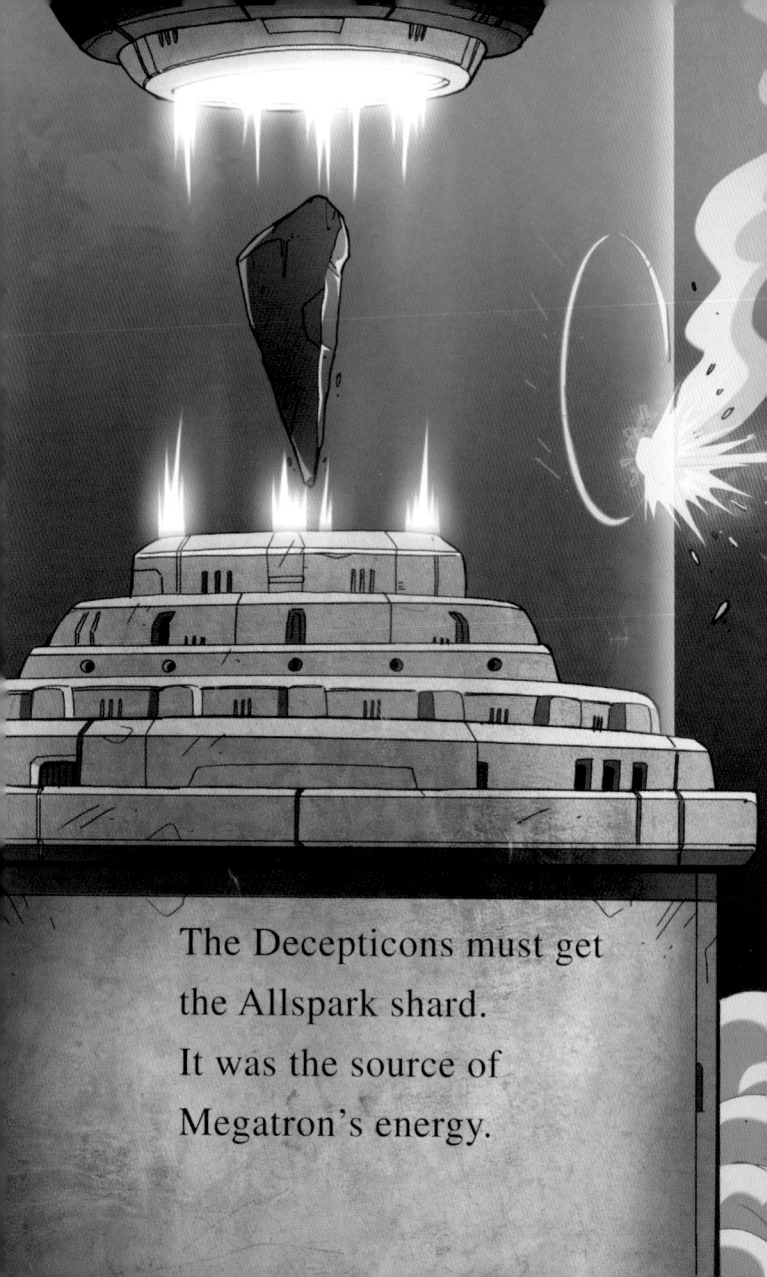

The Decepticons must get
the Allspark shard.
It was the source of
Megatron's energy.

The shard is in a locked vault.
Ravage outsmarts the humans.
He gets the shard!

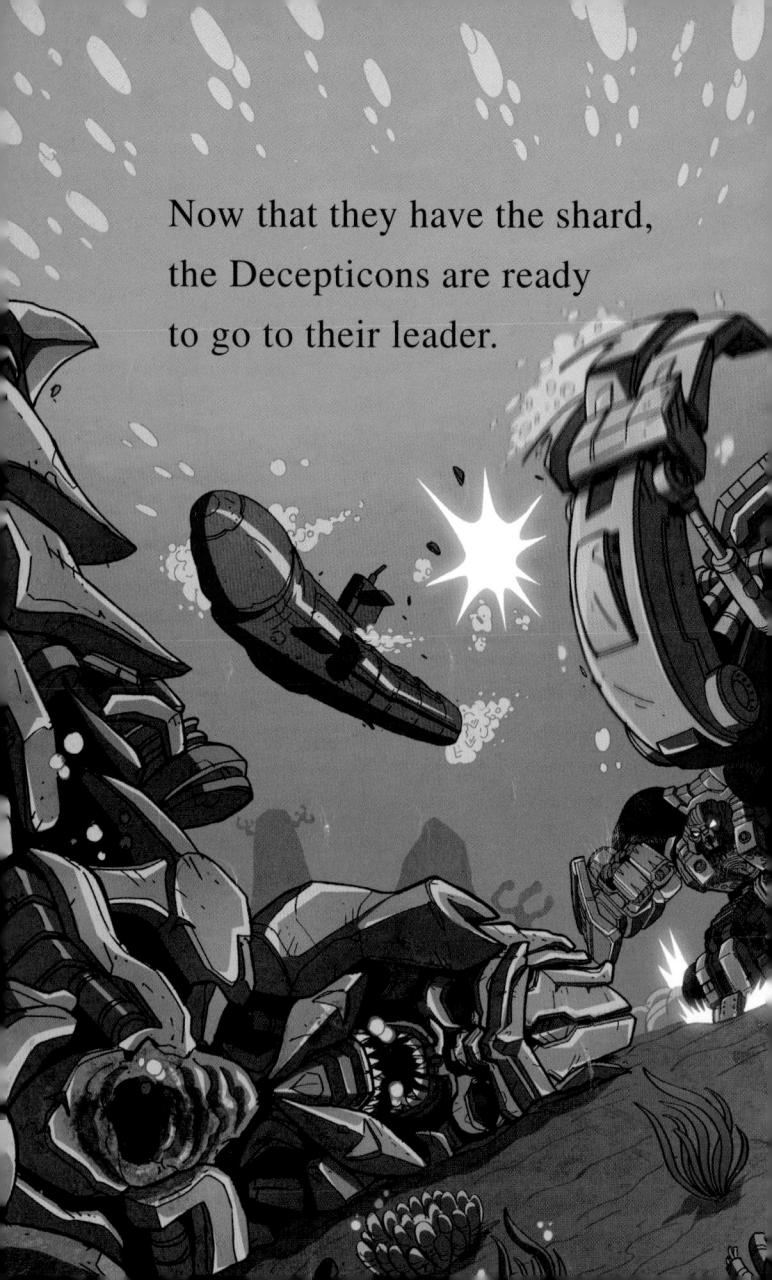

Now that they have the shard, the Decepticons are ready to go to their leader.

The Decepticons get past
the submarines.
The evil 'bots find Megatron.

The Doctor is a nimble 'bot.
Using his jointed arms,
the Doctor puts the shard
into Megatron.

Megatron bursts to life!
He's back and he's bad.

Now the good guys
have to watch out.
The battle for Earth
has never been harder.

Megatron is not alone.

His Decepticon army is by his side.

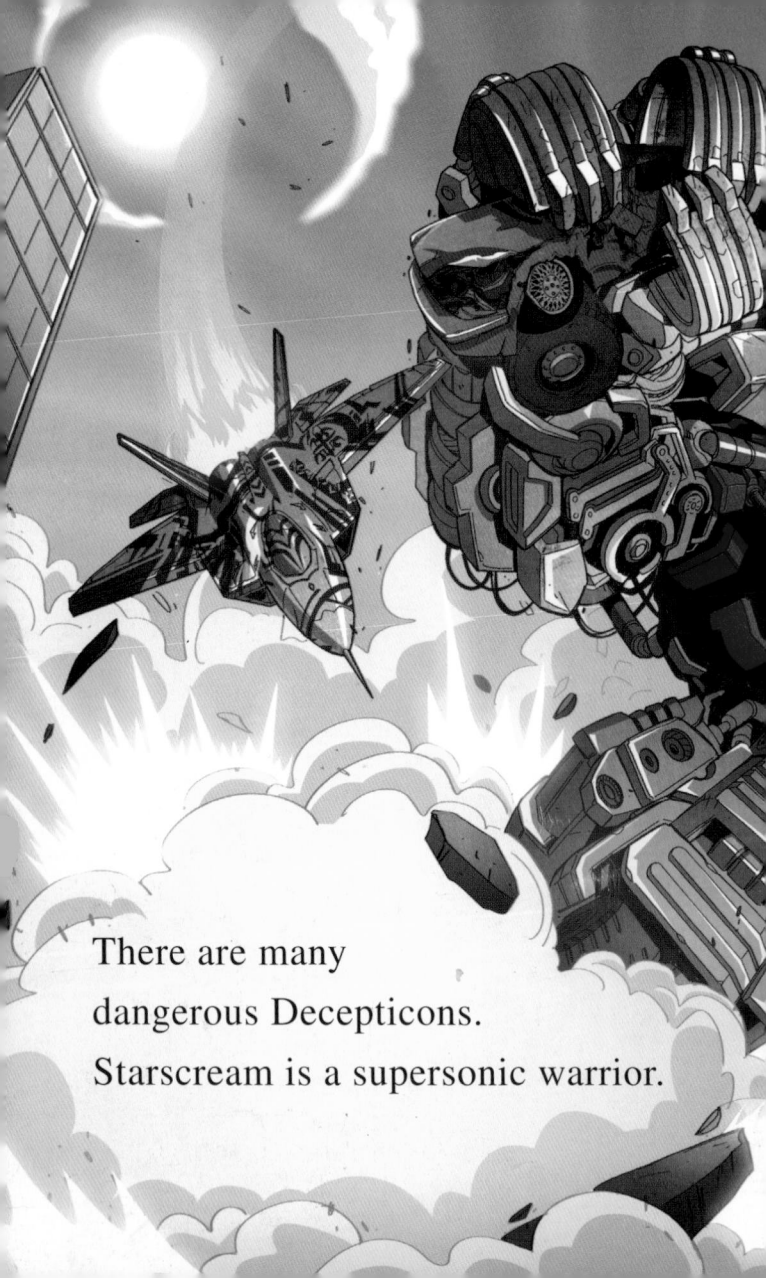

There are many
dangerous Decepticons.
Starscream is a supersonic warrior.

Devastator is one MEGA-bot!
He is a scary foe.

But the most evil Decepticon of all
is The Fallen.
The Fallen has been asleep
for ages.
Now he is back, and he is stronger
than ever!

The Autobots
and their human friends
prepare for one hard fight.

Luckily, the Autobots have
two secret weapons.
Wheels and Jetfire are Decepticons
who changed sides.

Now they fight for good
with Optimus Prime
and the Autobots.

Wheels is small,
but he is as brave
as the biggest 'bot.

Jetfire is old,
but he is still very powerful.
He is also very wise.

Can the Autobots beat
the Decepticons once again?

Or will Megatron and The Fallen
be too powerful?

Only one thing is sure:
Optimus Prime and his Autobots
will never give up!

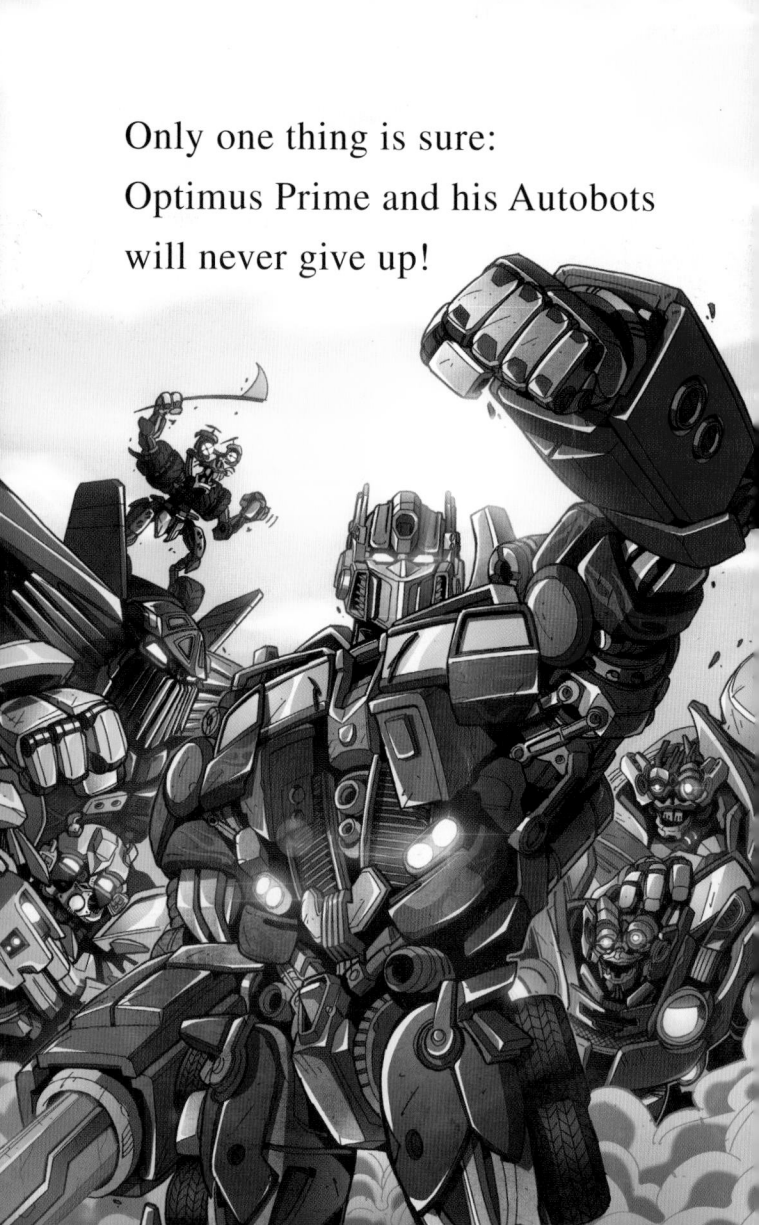

TRANSFORMERS
REVENGE OF THE FALLEN

I Am Optimus Prime

TRANSFORMERS
REVENGE OF THE FALLEN

I Am Optimus Prime

Adapted by Jennifer Frantz
Illustrations by Guido Guidi
Based on the Screenplay by
Ehren Kruger & Alex Kurtzman & Roberto Orci

Optimus Prime is the brave leader
of the Autobots.
They are robots in disguise!

Optimus is not just any 'bot.

He is the last of the great Primes,

a line of noble robots.

They come from

the planet Cybertron.

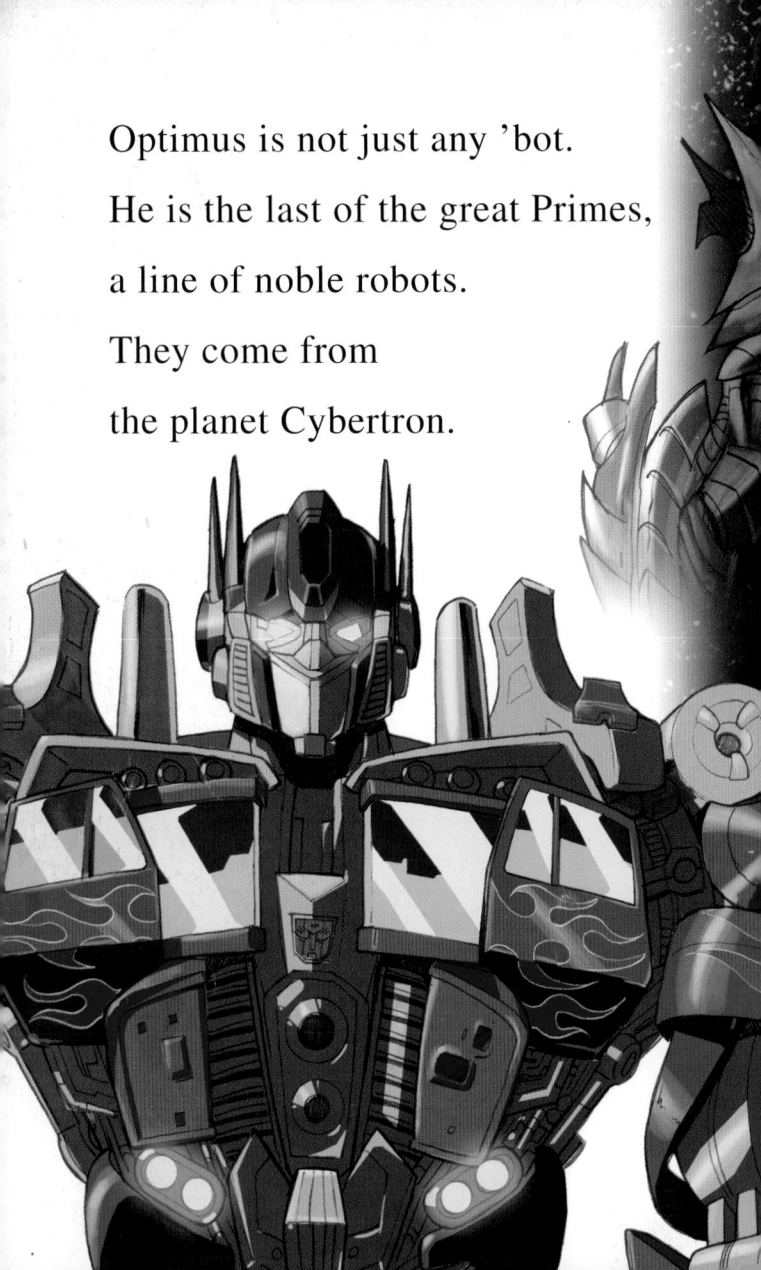

Like all true Primes,

Optimus fights for what is right.

Here on planet Earth,

Optimus Prime

is a friend to humans.

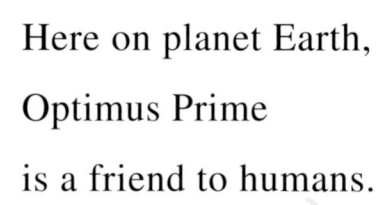

Side by side,

humans and Autobots battled Megatron

and his evil Decepticons.

Now Earth has a new threat.

And Optimus Prime has a new enemy.

The enemy's name is The Fallen.

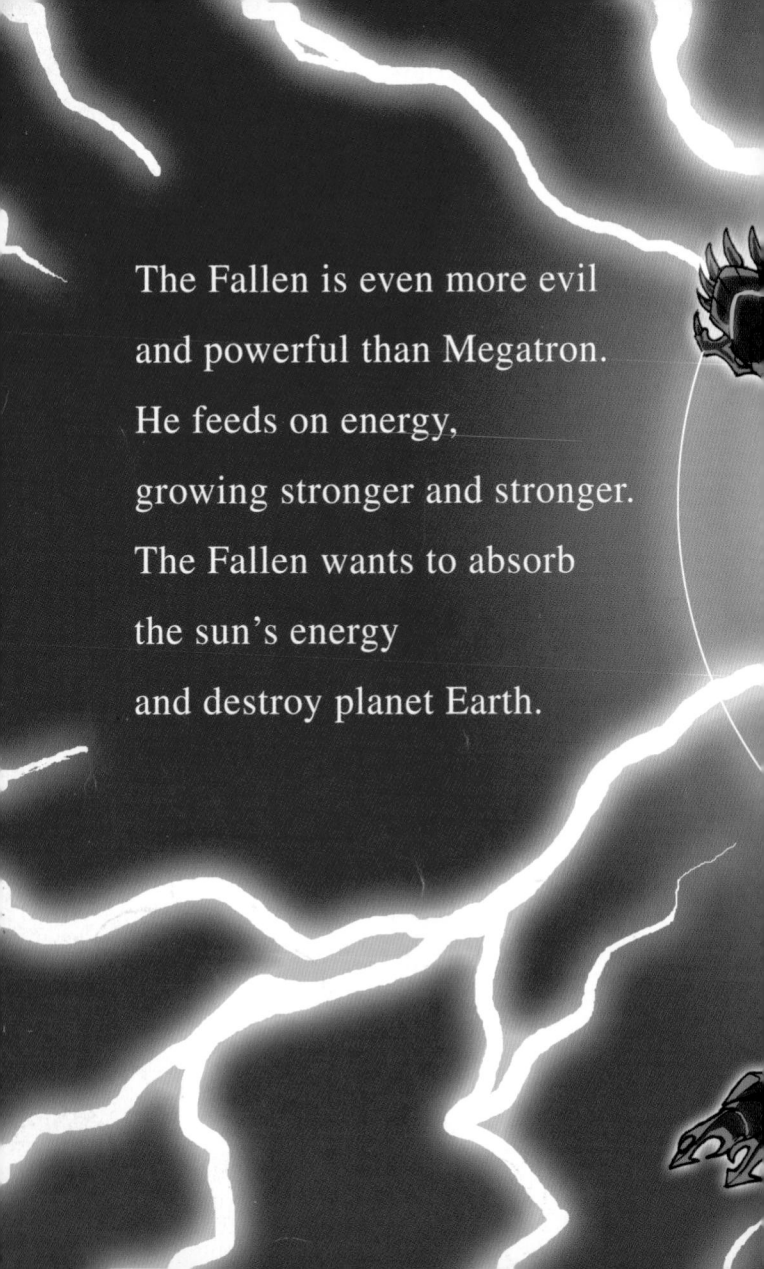

The Fallen is even more evil
and powerful than Megatron.
He feeds on energy,
growing stronger and stronger.
The Fallen wants to absorb
the sun's energy
and destroy planet Earth.

Optimus Prime must
stop The Fallen.
But he is not alone!

The brave Autobots are ready to do
whatever their leader asks.

Look out, Decepticons!
The Twins might look little
but they are double trouble.

Ironhide and Optimus Prime

make a great team.

Together they defeat the evil Demolisher.

Bumblebee is a loyal 'bot.

He will go anywhere

to help a friend.

Sideswipe is a fearless fighter.

He will do anything

for Optimus Prime.

The battle is on!
The Autobots face off
against the Decepticons.

Optimus Prime is ready to rumble!

Bumblebee blasts

a bulldozing Decepticon!

Bumblebee is small and fast.

Bumblebee has never fought better.

He wins this battle!

The Twins take on
the deadly Devastator.

This giant 'bot
is bad news!

In the end,

Optimus Prime sends The Fallen

screaming into space.

The sun is saved.

Optimus made the Earth safe

from Decepticons.

At least, for now.